Summer Solstice

WRITTEN BY
NICOLE W. BARNES

ISBN: 978-1-964619-67-5

Table of Contents

Introduction

Summer Solstice was inspired by the struggles faced in an abusive relationship. The author, Nicole Barnes, decided to write this fiction work as a way to help other women work through their trauma and show them that there is a way out.

The events in this book are comprised of the author's personal experiences. Names have been changed to protect those involved in the situations portrayed.

A Note from the Author

Dearest Reader,

I hope you find this story when you need it most. Years after my pain and heartache I have found the courage to write about it as a way to heal my heart and mind. It doesn't matter if it's been days, months, or years. The shadows of torment and abuse will always be there. Find your tribe. The ones that make you feel whole. Then, heal yourself. Take your time doing this. Rushing the healing process is no different than rushing physical therapy after surgery. And, again, it's an ache you will always feel.

I urge you to read my story with caution. Take breaks as needed, but let it show you that you aren't alone. I wouldn't be who I am today without my past, and neither are you. It will make you stronger, determined, broken, and bruised. But you **will** come out on top.

 Nicole W. Barnes

Part I

CHAPTER 1

How Did I Get Here?

"I'm not sure, Doc. I just woke up and decided it was finished. You keep asking me what pushed me over the edge, but I don't know how to answer that. I just...was ready."

Jen scrubbed her face with her palms. The friction caused her cheeks to turn red, but it was a soothing kind of burn. That was one thing her therapist hadn't picked up on yet. Jen found uncommon ways to dull her internal ache by causing herself discomfort that left no marks.

She was asked if self-harm ever came to mind, but to Jen, that was more of *really* hurting yourself. You know, like cutting to watch the blood trickle. Or smashing your hand on purpose just to feel the pain. She'd never done any of those things. To her, rubbing her skin and scratching her arm with a pushpin wasn't that.

Dr. Marsden looked at Jen over her tortoise-shell glasses. They were too big for her face, to be honest.

"Jennifer, I feel like you don't want to make progress on this topic today. Why don't we move on to something else? Something happier." She flipped a page on her notepad and started writing (what Jen saw as) random things.

"Maureen. Can I call you Maureen?" Without waiting, Jen continued, "I just decided I was done. I knew I couldn't continue to live that way anymore. Trying to pry a different answer out of me won't do any good. As a matter of fact, I think I'm better. I haven't had any panic attacks or bouts of anxiety in days." She slid back on the cool leather couch and crossed her arms over her chest.

"I suppose Maureen is fine since we've been seeing each other for a month now. Plenty of time to heal from the trauma you faced. Amiright?" It was Dr. Marsden's turn to lean back and fold her arms over her chest. She'd figured out that the best way to get Jen to crack was by facing her head on.

The two women stared at each other in silence. Jen was the first to look away. She didn't want Maureen to see her tears, even though she'd seen so many of them before that session.

Through a ragged breath, Jen spoke. "It was the miscarriage. That was the reason I left. He had no remorse for killing *my* baby, so I had no reason to stay after that."

She snatched a tissue from the floral box beside her and

covered her eyes. Dabbing wouldn't stop the tears from flowing. They always fell faster when she talked about her baby. She didn't even know what sex it was, but that didn't matter. What mattered was that Andrew made sure the baby didn't make it.

"I know this is hard for you, Jen. But if you don't face it head-on, it could be what drags you back into the dark hell you were in when you first came to see me." Maureen handed Jen a bottle of water and waited before she continued. "You're torturing yourself by not working through the loss of your baby. That's what Andrew would want. He wins. You can't let that happen." It wasn't often that Maureen spoke this way about a person, but this specific case led her to want to say so much more.

Once Jen was able to speak again, it was just above a whisper. "He doesn't win. I won't let him. I'll force myself through hell and high water before I let him see me this way. He. Won't. Win." Jen let the stone-cold hatred emanate from her eyes.

This was where Jen forced herself to not think of the past. She forced herself to think of all the good that had come from her leaving Andrew. It felt nice to start over in a new place. A place where no one knew anything about her or her past. She could be anyone she desired. And right now, at this moment, she wanted to be someone else. It was time to turn on the facade she had perfected while still with Andrew.

Jen tucked her hair behind her ears and met Maureen's eyes with the same softness. "I'm starting over. I'm learning to be happy again. I'm trying my damnedest to let all this go. Baby steps. Isn't that what you told me last time? Please don't make me take two steps back by pulling this out of me today. I'm exhausted."

Maureen closed the file that held notes on Jen's sessions. "I think we are out of time for today, Jen. Go rest and eat something healthy. Your gaunt face gives that away. You're far too beautiful to wither away to nothing. You can beat this. You've proven to me over and over just how strong you really are." She stood and held out a hand to help Jen from the couch.

Jen willingly took it and held on for a second longer than needed. "I'll do my best, Maureen." She slid her hand away and slowly turned to leave. She stopped at the door before glancing over her right shoulder. "Same time next week?"

Maureen nodded slightly as if to say *you know it* and softly smiled at Jen.

Jen returned the smile and walked out, quietly shutting the door behind her.

CHAPTER 2

Darkness Returns...

Jen made her way back to her motel room after stopping for food. The burger and fries from the local fast food joint were starting to get old, but at this point, it was all Jen could afford. The soggy fries with salt falling off of them were less than appetizing. The burger, well, that was another turn-up of her nose. Nothing was appealing anymore. Jen couldn't remember the last time she'd had a decent meal.

She forced down a few bites before throwing the rest into a bowl. There were a few stray cats that roamed around the motel. They looked just as homely as Jen, so she had to give them something. The owner, Mr. Blake, had given her a few sideways looks about it but didn't say anything. He must have accepted the fact that she wasn't going to stop since he had placed a water dish next to the one for food.

She walked out onto the patio and set the bowl down next to the water. Two small kittens ran over to greet her. She stooped down and gently rubbed their ears. This was a huge step from where they first started. She couldn't get close to them in the beginning without being hissed and spat at. She didn't dare name them, though. She knew that giving an animal a name meant that you were attached. She couldn't care for herself properly, let alone an animal.

Jen sat on the concrete and leaned up against the chain-link fence, watching the kittens fight over the remaining fries. A quiet chuckle escaped her lips just as she heard footsteps approaching from behind. Jen jumped to her feet and spun around to find Mr. Blake standing a few feet away.

"I didn't mean to scare you, Miss Jen. I know you asked for an extended stay, and I can still do that, but do you think you might want something more permanent?"

When Jen didn't answer, he continued. "My niece, Natalie, is a real estate agent in Prosperity. It's just the next town over, probably twenty minutes from here. She sends me listings that have been reduced or are at a low price for my tenants who need a long-term place. I'm not trying to push you out because you are a good one to keep around, but the resources are out there if you'd like to get in touch with her." He stuck his hands in the pockets of his jeans and rocked back on his heels.

Jen hesitated but decided to ask more about the opportunity. "When you say reduced or cheap, do you mean rundown and desolate? Not that it matters, but I'd like a general idea before contacting her." She tugged at the sleeves of her shirt, which was now way too big. She really did need to eat a sandwich.

Mr. Blake smiled at his partial victory. "I can show you the listings if you'd like. There are a few that need a lot of TLC, but also a few that are move-in ready." He still didn't move. Almost like Jen with the kittens when they first came around, he waited patiently for her to take the first step.

"I'd like that, Mr. Blake. I don't have a lot saved, but maybe it's enough to get my feet set somewhere nice." She started toward the office with Mr. Blake beside her. "And I don't think you'd let me jump into the ocean without a life vest. You've been good to me, and I truly appreciate it. I haven't felt that kindness in a long time." For the rest of the walk, each held a quiet understanding of the other.

They spent the next hour or so looking through the listings Natalie had sent him earlier that day. She liked three, but one stuck out to her the most. It had the most beautiful porch and yard. She asked Mr. Blake to print the listing and took down Natalie's phone number. She'd call when she had a better game plan, hoping the home wasn't scooped up by then.

"Goodnight, Miss Jen. Things are going to get better for you, whatever your story. You're good people." With that, he gently shut the office door behind her and switched on the *closed* sign.

Jen also returned to her room and slumped down onto the foot of the bed. So many things were running through her mind that she doubted she'd be able to sleep well. Getting up, she trudged to the bathroom to wash her face and brush her teeth. The person staring back at her wasn't the Jen she'd loved many years ago. Andrew had taken that from her before she left. A heavy sigh escaped her lips as she turned to get in bed. Even if she couldn't sleep, the things Mr. Blake talked with her about would be a good distraction. More quickly than she thought, her eyes drifted shut, and a restless sleep met Jen in the darkness.

Jen locked herself in the bathroom, hoping Andrew didn't get the wild hair to break the door down. He'd already tried once, and she didn't think it would hold if he tried again. She could hear him stomping back and forth from the bedroom to the kitchen. She wasn't sure what he was doing, but she knew she needed a barrier between them.

"Open the fucking door, Jen!" Andrew yelled from the other side. "Open! The! Fucking! Door!" he yelled again, each word spoken with a solid hit to the door between them.

Jen trembled but unlocked the door. She knew if she didn't, it would be worse when he got to her. She stilled herself as the knob slowly turned. Andrew didn't push the door open immediately, causing Jen's anxiety to shoot through the roof. She didn't dare pull it toward her, though. She wasn't crazy, regardless of what Andrew told everyone.

Andrew slowly let the door drift away from its frame until he was face-to-face with Jen. He didn't say anything, only gave her a shit-eating smirk. He stepped across the threshold and looked down his nose at her.

"You think you can get away with shutting me out in my own house? You don't have that authority. I pay the fucking rent on this piece of shit." He was close enough that she could smell the alcohol on his breath. "When I get back, I want it spotless in here. I better not be able to find a crumb on the floor. You hear me?" He didn't step back until Jen nodded her compliance.

At that, Andrew slung everything from the countertop onto the floor, breaking two bottles of his cologne and a vase holding the flowers he had just bought her yesterday. He then made his way to the kitchen, knocking all of the pictures off the wall on his way. The kitchen would be the place for him to unleash his full anger. He took the crockpot that had been cooking all day and smashed it to the floor. He then took every glass and threw them up against the refrigerator (luckily, most of them were plastic). He finished by flipping the table over. The burning candle slung melted wax across the window and into the new curtains.

"Now get started," Andrew simply stated as he slammed the front door shut behind him.

Jen waited for his truck to crank and speed down the road before crumbling into a heap in the middle of the kitchen floor. She could feel shards of glass claw at her legs. The smell of the now-out candle burned her nostrils. She shook, screamed, and cried for everything that she felt. The anger she couldn't let him see. The fear that coursed through her veins every time he was home. The sadness of her things being destroyed over and over again. But yet, she stayed.

Jen could never leave because no one else would want a broken, mentally unstable woman in her thirties. Andrew was all she had, and he knew it. Despite all his flaws, she still loved him. She prayed every day that he would change his ways and love her back. He said he did, but that didn't mean much. Hell, they were engaged, but the ring meant nothing to him. It was just a ploy to get Jen to come home the last time she left.

She wasn't strong enough to go. She didn't have enough money to find another place. She didn't even have a car to take her somewhere else. Everything in her life had fallen apart at the hands of the man she loved. Yet, she still stayed.

CHAPTER 3

All Good Things...

The next morning, Jen called Dr. Marsden, or Maureen, and scheduled a much-needed session.

"I can't get you in until after closing, Jen. I'll have to run it as an emergency session, and like I said when we started, that could cost more than a normal session. It depends on how long it takes. I'm generous to give my clients twenty minutes of free time after hours, but I have a family to get home to." She sighed at Jen's silence. "Look, you don't take advantage of this like some others, so I'll cut you a break this time. For you to call after the way we ended yesterday, it must be something heavy. I'll see you around 5:30?"

Jen covered her face with her free hand and clenched the phone with the other. "Doc, you're an angel. I'll be there at 5:15." She tapped the end button and dropped the phone onto her still-unmade bed.

She didn't have to work today but needed to stay busy, so

she offered to help Mr. Blake clean some rooms. This was a win-win for both of them. He got clean rooms, and she got to keep idle hands at bay. Jen snapped the rubberband she kept on her wrist and stood to make her way to the bathroom. A shower might help wash away the sleepless night.

She turned on the water and waited for it to warm up. "Scalding. Just the way I like it," she whispered to herself." Jen stepped under the hell water and let it rinse away her aches and misery.

By noon, Jen had already tackled five rooms. Mr. Blake told her she worked too fast but that he liked her efficiency. He walked out of the office with a tray holding a ham sandwich, some chips, and a soda. He placed it on the patio table and waited for Jen to come out of the room she was finishing up in.

"I fixed you lunch, Miss Jen. It's the least I can do for you helping me out on your days off." He slid his hands into his pocket and rocked back on his heels, the same as every time he spoke without the desk in front of him. It was a quirk that Jen took to mean he wasn't too comfortable with conversations.

"Thank you, Mr. Blake. Join me for a few minutes?" She motioned to the chair next to hers and sat down gently. She didn't trust these chairs too much. She'd seen them throw many patrons over the past few weeks.

Mr. Blake nodded and sat, not quite as gingerly as Jen. He couldn't seem to sit still; he rocked the chair and began twiddling his thumbs. "I'm not trying to pry, but have you given any more thought to calling my niece?"

Jen finished the bite of the sandwich in her mouth before replying, "Yes, sir, I have. I actually have it on my list to do after I finish up the last two rooms." She wiped her mouth with a napkin and continued, "Do you really think she can help me find a place? I mean, I don't have much to stand on as far as credit goes, and I don't have a whole lot saved up, but I have some, and I can get more for reassurance of paying the mortgage." She paused for a breath. She realized she was rambling, which she often did when she was nervous. Jen shrugged her shoulders and looked down like a defeated child.

At this, Mr. Blake stopped rocking and leaned onto the table between them. "Miss Jen, she's been in your shoes before. She knows what it's like to need a break in order to get back on your feet. If anyone can help you, it's her." He stood and wiped his hands on the legs of his pants. "Now, if you'll excuse me, I have some filing to do. Thank you again for all of your help."

Jen smiled and sat back confidently in the metal chair. She

even felt brave enough to kick her feet up on the railing. The chair seemed sturdy enough until it quickly jolted backward, trying to throw her to the ground. She shot up out of the seat and quickly turned to look at it.

"You're not going to ruin my day, you stupid piece of shit." She kicked the chair, catching her shoelace on the leg. Tripping backward and falling on her butt, she laughed. "Okay, maybe I deserved that." After a minute, she stood and brushed herself off. Grabbing her cleaning cart, she started down the walkway.

"Let's knock out these last two so I can call this Natalie lady."

Jen cleaned herself up in her room before sitting in the armchair next to the window. This one she could trust. She shuffled papers on her desk and found the ones Mr. Blake had given her with Natalie's information. She dialed the number and stared at the phone. Pressing the call button would mean yet another life-changing decision. Was she ready for that? She locked the phone and laid it on the desk. She closed her eyes and thought back on the past few years.

She met Andrew through mutual friends at a lake house one summer. He was new in town and had all the girls drooling after him on his jet ski. The new guys always had that effect in a small town. He was broad-shouldered with sandy blonde hair, tanned skin, and green eyes. He looked to be a few years younger than Jen, but she always seemed drawn to the younger ones. Next to the beauties in their late teens and early twenties, she didn't stand a chance. She threw back her beer and finished the bottle before standing to go floating off the dock.

At peace, she let the wake of passing boats draw her float out some. With it being tied to the pillar, she knew she'd be fine. Daydreaming in the warm sun was one thing she selfishly took advantage of. It wasn't for a tan; she was as pale as a porcelain doll. It just felt nice.

Before she knew it, someone was floating next to her. The pop of a can tab was her clue. She looked in the direction of the sound and was surprised to see Andrew holding a beer in her direction.

"Hi, mind if I join you?" he said simply, with a smirk that showed his dimples.

Jen cooly took the can and replied, "With the offering of a beer, of course you can."

The conversation ran smoothly throughout the afternoon. Andrew really was as smooth as they made him out to be. Almost too smooth for Jen to fall for his good-boy charm. Almost...next thing she knew, they were headed to his truck to go out for dinner. Oh, how the younger girls cut their eyes at them. Glorious victory! Jen couldn't help but revel in their jealousy. She never got the guy.

Jen shook herself from her daydream and looked at the clock. *Shit!* It was already 5:00. She grabbed her room keys and ran out the door. She still didn't have a car, but luckily, everything in this town was within a stone's throw. She ran the two blocks to Maureen's office and waited for her in the lobby. This time, she took advantage of the water cooler. She was definitely out of shape and needed to run more often. It was a hobby from her past that she longed to do again.

Not five minutes later, Maureen walked into the lobby with her file in hand and held the door to her office open for Jen. Maureen crossed to the exterior door, locked it, and drew the curtain.

"We have all the time you need, Jen. I promise, you have my undivided attention. And all the tissues in the office are at your disposal." She chuckled at her own joke and shook her head at Jen's humored eye roll.

"Shall we?" She closed the office door and settled into the armchair as Jen stretched out on the couch.

CHAPTER 4

Come Crashing Down...

Jen closed her eyes and let the soft classical music take her away from her thoughts. Maureen had more figured out about Jen than she thought. This music was what got her to relax and feel at peace with the world. Apparently, Maureen thought it would get her to open up also.

"How has today been for you, Jen?" Maureen asked as she flipped pages in her notepad. This one was stuck in Jen's file, so it must be all about her. "Hopefully better after whatever prompted you to call?"

Jen peeked at her from the corner of her left eye, hoping to avoid answering altogether. Maureen cleared her throat, so Jen reluctantly sat up and sank back into the cushions. She kicked off her shoes and pulled her knees to her chest.

"I had another flashback yesterday. It took me into my dark place again." She snapped the rubberband on her wrist. "It was a bad one this time." Another snap on her wrist, a little harder this time.

Maureen wrote something on her notepad and rested her hands on top of it when she was finished. "Does it have anything to do with what we discussed yesterday? Your reason for leaving?" *Snap*... Another mark was made on the notepad.

Jen rested her forehead on her knees and sighed heavily. She gave a whispered answer this time. "Yes." That was all she could get out at the moment.

She threw her head back in frustration at the silence. Maureen never gave when she knew Jen could give more. *Snap*... Another mark.

"You know, Doc, this game of not really helping me talk things out is really getting old. I thought that was what you were supposed to do." Jen waited again, staring hard at Maureen. "Fine. I'll talk, but only if there's absolutely no judgment or any words spoken until I'm finished."

Maureen nodded in agreement, and Jen continued. She stretched out on the couch again, only this time covering her eyes with her arm. The complete blackness would make it easier for her to disconnect.

Jen walked into the house after work to find it a total disaster again and Andrew sleeping in the recliner. She didn't dare wake him. At least not until she'd tidied up some. She gathered clean clothes that had been dumped on the floor of the laundry room and began to fold them. She then put them away and started another load. She made her way to the kitchen to find the meat she took out that morning back in the freezer. Apparently, Andrew didn't want pork chops tonight. Jen opened the cabinets to find something quick and easy since it was after 6:00 on a Friday. Everywhere in town would be packed, and there was no way she'd be able to leave without Andrew blowing a fuse.

She pulled out a box of Zatarain's Jambalaya rice and smoked sausage. This always went over well, so why not, she thought. As soon as the food finished cooking, Andrew walked into the kitchen. He stirred the food and fixed his plate without a word. Jen followed suit, and they sat together at the table in silence.

Jen picked at her meal, but Andrew ate quickly. He left his dishes on the table for her to clear and got in the shower. Jen closed her eyes tightly, knowing this meant he would be leaving soon. She wasn't sure if she felt relief or the constant disappointment that he didn't want to spend time with her. She dumped her remaining food into the trash and put away the leftovers for another day. She had to handwash the dishes since Andrew refused to fix the dishwasher. He said a good housewife *would wash things by hand to make sure they were spotless for her man.*

Jen was putting the last of the dishes away just as Andrew came stomping down the hall in his heavy boots. He left a cloud of strong cologne behind him. Jen stifled a cough and turned to look at him. Andrew was wearing new jeans and his favorite yellow polo. No hat, because it would mess up his perfectly styled shaggy hair. He looked coldly at Jen as if to ask what the hell she wanted.

"You look nice," was all Jen dared to say. Even then, she wasn't sure if he'd get angry and pick a fight. When he didn't respond, she decided to go a little further. "Can I expect you home tonight? Or do I need to go ahead and lock everything up?"

At this, Andrew was in her face in a heartbeat. Jen didn't dare let him see the fear she felt. "Why the hell does it matter to you? You got your boyfriend coming over while I'm gone?" It was even more unnerving that he whispered it.

Jen lifted her chin and quietly shook her head no. She knew words would be her undoing. She looked Andrew in the eye until he stormed off and grabbed his keys from the hook. He slung the lamp from the end table and slammed the door behind him.

Jen waited until the truck was no longer heard and crumpled to the floor. This time, the tears didn't fall. It was almost as if she was numb to it all now. It had been two years of this. Well, one and a half since he used the first six months to move in and make her fall for him. Those six months were the best relationship Jen had ever been in. Andrew would take her out, show her off, and even stay home to spend time with her. Then, he slowly started to unwind.

Andrew started by going out with the boys for the night here and there. Then it turned into him sneaking out when he thought she was asleep. That turned into his phone being locked with a crazy puzzle-type code and always by his side. He would randomly leave to go to the gas station and just never come back. It eventually turned into Andrew being more of a bad roommate than a boyfriend.

Jen found out through the local gossip chain that he had been cheating on her. This didn't do anything but solidify her suspicions. She confronted him about it once, but that turned into a knock-down drag-out between the two of them.

Andrew had wrestled her to the floor and shoved his knee into her chest. When she turned purple from not being able to breathe, he shoved her down again before getting up. He sat on the couch with a triumphant look on his face, only for Jen to go after him. She scratched at him and spit in his face. He slapped her hard across her cheek and threw her into the hope chest they *had refurbished together during the first six months.*

The impact caused Jen to shake uncontrollably. It was almost as if Andrew himself had entered a state of panic because he snatched her up from the floor and dropped her into the bathtub. He turned on the cold water and dumped it over Jen's head as she heaved from the pain.

"This is dumb, Jen! Look what you made me do to you. You should've never started this shit! Why do you always make me do things you end up regretting?" He yelled the entire time, but Jen couldn't hear the words. The ringing in her ears just got louder and louder until everything turned black.

Jen stopped talking and let the tears flow freely. Maureen was now at her side, sitting on the floor. She dabbed at Jen's face with the tissues and rubbed her arm soothingly. Jen made no move to uncover her eyes or even open them. She had given Maureen more trust than she had anyone in the past few years. She sobbed silently and let Maureen continue to comfort her. It felt nice to have someone care, even if that person was paid to do it.

After the sobs subsided, Jen sat and took a sip of water from the bottle Maureen had set beside her at some point during the session. "I'm so sorry, Doc. I don't know what came over me. I'm a blubbering mess." She wiped her face again with the tissues and sat with her knees to her chest.

Maureen gave a tiny smile and whispered, "This is what you need, Jen. This is the breakthrough to start your healing. Whatever caused you to open up is a blessing. It may not feel like it right now, but it is. Baby steps." Maureen sat back in the chair across from Jen and placed the notepad back on her lap.

Snap... Another mark on the notepad.

"What do you keep writing? It's not sentences because you're not writing for very long." Jen knew Maureen probably wouldn't tell her, but she asked anyway.

Snap... Another mark.

"Are you aware that you snap your wrist with that rubberband?" It was as if Jen didn't even realize she was doing it.

Jen looked down and pulled on the rubberband but didn't let it go this time. "Oh...that. I have it to try to distract my mind from thoughts like what I just told you. It's soothing to me."

"You have snapped it seventeen times since you walked in the door. It was more frequent while you were talking. What's the connection with Andrew and the snapping?" Maureen sat a little straighter, waiting for Jen to answer.

Instead, Jen stood up and threw her tissues in the trash. "Thank you, Doc, for meeting with me again. I truly appreciate it. I'll let you get home to your family." Before Maureen could respond, Jen was out the door and making her way back to the motel.

Snap... Snap... Snap... Snap...

The snapping continued all the way back to her room. Mr. Blake wasn't outside this evening, so she didn't have to make small talk. She unlocked her door with shaky hands and leaned up against it once it was closed.

Snap... Snap...

Her phone let out a shrill ring into the silence, causing Jen to jump. She pulled it from her pocket only to see *Andrew* on the screen. She threw her phone across the room and slid to the floor.

"There's no way he's found me," Jen whispered to herself. "I didn't leave any leads. How could he know?" Sobs wracked her body again until she fell into a fitful sleep on the floor.

CHAPTER 5

Andrew...

Jen was awakened by a gentle tapping at her door. The pain of sleeping on the floor seemed to delay her response to answering. She stood and placed her hand on the knob before remembering the terrifying call she had gotten the night before. *Andrew...*

Jen looked through the peephole and saw only Mr. Blake. He didn't look up at the door, only to his left towards his office. "She may not be awake yet, sir. Is there something I can possibly help you with?"

Sir? Someone was with him at her door. She snatched her hand back from the knob as if it had just shocked her. There was no way she was opening the door now. The shrill ring of her phone caused her to jump back towards the door. She was stuck in the middle like a mouse being toyed with by a pair of angry alley cats. She stretched her neck to look at the screen. *Andrew...*

Dammit! He had found her. But how? She tiptoed to the door again and peeked out, only to be met with Andrew's face this time. A jolt of lightning shook her body. Once the trembling started, there was no way she could get it to stop. She sat on her bed, staring at the door. What was she supposed to do now? How did she get herself into this mess? There was no one that knew where she was, not even her family. She didn't dare contact them until she was sure Andrew was long over her leaving.

She could hear muffled voices from the porch but couldn't make out what they were saying. She snatched up her phone and silenced it before it could ring again. *Rookie mistake...*

After the ringing didn't sound, the banging on her door started. Once that didn't work, the yelling ensued, "Open the door, Jen! I know you're in there!" Another round of banging, and then the guilt trip... "You owe me an explanation, baby. You left me with a broken heart and no way of knowing you were safe." A few more moments of silence before, "OPEN THE FUCKING DOOR!" Andrew had lost his cool in public this time.

"Sir, I'm going to have to ask you to leave the premises. Obviously, Miss Ashworth isn't in, or she would've opened the door for you." Mr. Blake was stern yet very professional in his demand.

Andrew slammed his fist against the door one more time for good measure before going after Mr. Blake. "Look, old man. *Miss Ashworth* is my girlfriend. She left me with nothing. The bitch took everything I had and disappeared. I've come to get it *and* her back. Now, if you'll excuse me, I have a door to break down." And with that, Andrew started wailing on the door again.

Natalie thought her barrier was about to give up when she heard sirens in the parking lot. *Thank you, God...* Jen didn't know what to do other than thank the good Lord for those blue lights and sirens.

"I'm fucking leaving. But I'll be back for what's mine. You can count on that, old man." Andrew stomped off the porch to his truck while throwing his hands up at the cops. They couldn't do anything with him willingly leaving, and he knew that. He got in his truck and sped away.

The next knock on Jen's door was one from an officer. "Ma'am, this is Officer Richards. Can you open the door for me?"

Jen slowly turned the deadbolt and slid the slide lock off its latch plate. She slowly opened the door and refused to make eye contact with anyone. "Thank you, Officer, for getting him to leave. Is there a report being made?"

"Ma'am, are you okay? Can I get you anything?" Officer Richards used the voice Jen knew was reserved for the families of victims. She'd heard it before when she'd had Andrew arrested for holding her hostage in their house.

Jen looked up into the softest blue eyes she'd ever seen. They held a concern she'd never witnessed before. "Yes, sir, I'm okay. Just a little shaken up. I don't need anything other than a stiff drink right now." She hoped joking would take the edge off her anxiety.

Like magic, Mr. Blake appeared holding out a glass with an amber liquid and a few cubes of ice. "The finest whiskey I have, Miss Jen." His eyes were a steely gray. Not the kind ones she'd seen since meeting him. "Paul, I'll tell you right now. If that fella comes back, he won't be leaving on two feet." Mr. Blake turned and stomped back to his office, letting the door slam behind him.

Jen let a loving smile touch her face as she slowly sniffed the whiskey. She touched the glass to her lips and let the first sip warm her soul. "Please, Officer, have a seat. I'll answer any questions you have." Her trembling had started to subside as the whiskey started taking effect. Unfortunately, before Officer Richards could ask his first question, Jen heard the sound she would never be able to forget. Andrew's truck was coming this way.

The trembling started again as she sat the glass on the table. Officer Richards took notice and stood with his hand on his gun. "He's crazy if he turns in this lot again." The sound of the truck slowed as he made eye contact with Andrew. Neither dared to look away. Paul raised his chin and unsnapped the loop that held his gun in place. Out of his peripheral, he could see Jen pull her knees to her chest and cover her ears. *She's been through this before.* Paul knew a victim of abuse without them ever saying the words. His mother had lived the same way for far too long. The truck picked up speed again as it passed the driveway. Paul snapped the gun back in place and sat to look at Jen.

"Miss Ashworth, if I can promise you one thing, it's that he won't be in this town long. Is there a reason he's harassing you like this?" He knew the answer before it was even given.

Jen looked up, this time with tears running down her face. "He's my ex-boyfriend. When I left, I took $273 from his safe. It's all I took, I swear. I can pay it back if that's what I need to do. Just make him leave." She covered her ears again and sobbed.

Paul looked down at the beautiful woman trembling in

front of him. Clearly, she was scared of the asshole. Maybe even afraid for her life. He stooped down in front of her and leveled her eyes with his. "I will do everything in my power to keep him away from you." He stood and walked to his car. His only plan of action was to find something on this Andrew guy. Anything. He pulled the radio and called for any available officers to be on the lookout for the truck. It was a slow day, so they were all willing and ready to pull Andrew over.

Mr. Blake walked over to Paul's patrol car with a piece of paper in his hand. "I asked for his license when he came in. He handed it over with no issue. My policy to ID is clearly posted. His name is Andrew Clark. His address was from a few states away. Means Miss Jen ran pretty far to get away from him." Mr. Blake fiddled with the paper for a bit before continuing, "Anyway, here's the information I have. I pulled the cameras and also got his license plate for you." He rocked back on his heels and turned to walk away, shoving his hands in his pockets.

Paul flicked the edge of the paper with his finger before calling for Mr. Blake to stop. He met him halfway before continuing his questions. "You said she ran from him. What did you mean by that? Scared for her life? Has he threatened her before, to your knowledge?"

Mr. Blake looked down at the dirt and scrubbed the sand

with the toe of his shoe. "I don't have any proof other than the video from the day she came in here looking for a place to stay. She had a really bad bruise on her cheek and some marks on her arms. Almost like she'd been grabbed real hard? She kept looking over her shoulder and was very timid. I would have asked more questions, but I didn't want her to be scared off. This is a safe place, you know."

Paul nodded his agreement. "She's not the first runner you've been able to help. Can I get some of that footage? It may be able to help with a restraining order, if nothing else. If she was that scared, I doubt she has pressed charges before."

The two gentlemen shook hands, and Mr. Blake went to his office to download what he could. Paul flicked the edge of the paper with his finger some more before deciding to approach Jen again.

"Miss Ashworth, can I sit with you for a moment? I have some rather personal questions to ask you about this Andrew fellow." He waited for her nod before taking the seat next to her. "Has he threatened you in the past?"

Jen nodded.

"Has he physically hurt you in the past?" Paul asked with caution.

Jen nodded.

"Did you come here to hide from him?" Paul felt like he was walking on eggshells.

Jen closed her eyes and gave a heavy sigh. She nodded.

"Last question for now. Have you pressed charges on him before?" Paul held back the urge to hold her hand.

A single tear fell down Jen's cheek. She made no effort to wipe it away; she just let it fall. Jen nodded but then opened her mouth to speak. "I did, but I dropped them soon after. Like always, he promised things would get better. And they did, for a little while, anyway. I should've known better after years of putting up with his shit." She brought her knees up to her chest and buried her face in them. This was when she let the tears pour from her eyes. Her soul needed this. All of the pain, the hurt, the self-doubt was rushing from her body. She knew this was it for her and Andrew. She knew it when she left, but this solidified that action.

Paul didn't say anything; he just sat and let Jen feel everything and nothing all at once. He didn't know her, but he felt the urge to keep her safe. And that's what he'd do for as long as she was in town. He wasn't sure if Jen was just passing through or thinking of staying, but her safety net of a no-name town had disappeared in just a few hours. He'd help her feel safe again. If she would let him, that is.

CHAPTER 6

Paul...

The morning slowly faded, and the afternoon turned grey. The forecast called for showers and mild winds. Jen had made her way back into her room to rest and wash away the torment from her past. The officer from earlier stayed in his patrol car at the entrance of the parking lot. *He seems nice,* Jen thought to herself. She peeked out the curtains again just in time to see him walking towards the motel.

Paul glanced in her direction, but Jen didn't close the curtains. Their eyes met and held for a few seconds. *Damn, she's beautiful. Dumbasses ruin it for everyone.* He shook his head and looked down at his shoes while he continued to make his way to the office. Mr. Blake would be pleased to hear that Andrew Clark had been detained. Drinking and driving with possession of a weapon with no permit. *Dumbass... Paul* spat at the thought of Andrew and his behavior.

He knocked and asked Mr. Blake to step onto the porch.

"Mr. Blake, I just wanted to let you know that the threat of Mr. Clark returning is no more. He made the mistake of drinking and driving, which led to an altercation during the traffic stop. A simple search of his vehicle led to the discovery of a handgun that Mr. Clark did not have a permit for." He sighed and continued, "Miss Ashworth doesn't have to worry about him bothering her for a few days. Being it's the weekend, he will be locked up until Monday at the earliest."

Mr. Blake shook Paul's hand. "Thank you, Paul. You've always been a good kid. Why don't you let Miss Jen know the good news? I don't think it will be as comforting coming from a lowly old motel manager." He grinned and rocked back on his heels.

Paul nodded, getting what Mr. Blake meant. "Yes, sir. I'll let her know now." He turned towards Jen's room door before turning back. "Mr. Blake, do you think she'd like to get a warm meal with me?" He shoved his hands in his pockets and felt his cheeks flush.

"Well, son, everyone needs to eat. I wouldn't suggest anything too formal or crowded; she's not the showy type. Maybe grab a pizza or a few burgers and enjoy the swings by the fire pit. I've seen her out there scribbling away in a notebook." Mr. Blake patted Paul on the shoulder and went back into his office.

Paul slowly made his way to Jen's door, rehearsing what to say with each step. He knew she was fragile. He also knew that she was strong enough to get away from a bad situation. He wasn't confident she'd accept his offer, but he figured he'd give it a shot. *Knock, knock...* Paul waited patiently for Jen to answer. He could hear her walking towards the door and fiddling with the locks.

"Miss Ashworth, it's just me, Paul Richards. I have an update for you on the situation." *Too formal, Paul,* he thought to himself. "What I mean is you can rest easy for a while."

The door slowly opened, showing a puffy-faced Jen. "Is he gone or just hasn't been seen, and it's assumed he's left town?" She was too used to Andrew's games to believe he had actually left.

"He's in jail for the weekend at least. He was pulled over for reckless driving that turned out to be a DUI." Paul rubbed the back of his neck with his left hand as he hesitated to tell Jen the rest. "After he tussled with an officer, his truck was searched, and they found a weapon." He looked into her eyes for any hint of fear or relief.

Jen hugged herself and gave Paul the same gentle stare he had set on her. "He lost his permit the last time he was arrested. Does that make it a felony?”

Paul nodded hesitantly, “In a sense, yes. But I don’t want you to be concerned with that. I just want you to understand that you are safe, and I intend to keep it that way.” He shoved his hands back in his pockets and looked down at his shoes again before continuing. “Miss Ashworth, it’s been a long day, and I know you haven’t eaten anything. Is it too much to ask you to join me for a warm meal?”

Jen was caught off guard by the question, so she didn’t answer immediately. “Dinner? You’d like to go to dinner with *me*?” He seemed like a great guy and a very dedicated officer, but she’d heard too many stories of officers also being the villain. But at this point, what could it hurt? “Let me get my jacket and purse. I could definitely use a hot meal and a cup of good coffee.”

She left the room door open as she grabbed her things. *He couldn’t be a bad cop. Not after he sat here all day and made sure Andrew was taken into custody.*

Paul waited for her to exit the room and walked beside her, placing her on the side closest to the building. “We can take my patrol car or ride separately if you’d like.” He placed his hand gently on the small of her back as they made their way down the three steps leading to the parking lot.

Jen flinched slightly at his touch but played it off as a shiver. *Old habits die hard.* "We will have to take yours. I don't have a vehicle yet." She slid her jacket on as they rounded to the passenger side of the newer model sedan.

Paul opened the door for Jen and waited for her to be fully seated before closing it and walking around the back to get into the driver's seat. He slid in and made sure she was comfortable before starting towards the diner in town. It was only a few blocks, but the ride was made in silence.

Once parked at the diner, Jen opened her door but was stopped by Paul placing his hand on her left one. "I'll get that for you," he said as he quickly made his way back around to her side. "I apologize if it's a bit much, but my mom would have a fit if I didn't do it for you." He chuckled under his breath,

Jen smiled her first genuine smile in a long time.

CHAPTER 7

A Little High...

Jen sat in the lobby, waiting for Maureen to appear from her current session. She tapped her foot on the tile floor, unable to sit still. There was so much she needed to tell her that Jen felt she was about to burst at the seams.

When she heard footsteps approaching the lobby, Jen stood and willed herself not to push past the patient Maureen was walking out of her office.

"Hi, Jen. Right on time, as usual," Maureen smiled as she waved goodbye to the other patient.

"I have so much to tell you." Jen hurried to the office and perched herself on the edge of the couch. "The past few days have been hell, to say the least."

Maureen followed suit and seated herself on the chair closest to Jen. She placed the file and notepad on her lap and held the pen expectantly.

Without any more prompting, Jen began. "So, yesterday,

Andrew somehow found me. I'm still not quite sure how, but he showed up at my motel room. Mr. Blake wouldn't let him in and stood nearby while Andrew was there. Once Andrew realized that I wasn't letting him in either, he lost it. It was like being right back in the house with him screaming at me to *open the fucking door.*"

She paused for a breath and took a sip of water. "Well, the cops showed up and made him leave. This one officer, Officer Richards, stuck around the motel to make sure Andrew didn't come back. They ended up pulling him over somewhere in town and had grounds to arrest him."

Maureen raised her eyebrows but didn't speak a word. She took notes feverishly, hoping to find some sort of tactic to help Jen heal.

Jen took another breath and closed her eyes. "Last night, I had the first decent night's sleep I've had in years." She sank back into the couch and just let the tears flow. She wasn't sure how to put all of her feelings into words, but she knew Maureen understood.

Maureen had never seen Jen so vulnerable, but that wasn't necessarily a bad thing. Jen needed to release the tension and anger, and it may just be what she needed to become herself again. She sat in silence and waited.

Snap...

Maureen made a tally mark in her notes.

Jen cried for what seemed to be hours. When she opened her eyes again, she realized it had only been twenty minutes. "Maureen, I'm not sure I'll be able to stand it when he gets out. I was told they can only hold him 'til he posts bail, and I know it'll be as soon as his mom can get to him. What do I do?"

Maureen put her notepad on the coffee table and sat beside Jen on the couch. "You stay. You stay, and you hold your ground. Being a textbook narcissist, Andrew is using this tactic to try to get you to go back with him. He let his true colors show, but none of us know his past or motives. That only matters where you're from."

Snap...

Maureen wrote another tally before continuing, "He may be totally different once he's released, and try to put it off as him being hurt by your actions. You have made so much progress. In my opinion, as a friend, don't go back." She rubbed Jen's back as the silence continued.

Snap...

Another tally mark.

Jen looked at Maureen with a little glimmer of hope in her eyes. "Do you think I'm strong enough?"

She looked like a lost child, wanting acceptance and love. Maureen couldn't help it; she wrapped Jen in a tight hug and cried along with her.

After a few moments, the two women dried their tears.

Maureen felt led to ask, "How do you feel about the situation? With the police and Mr. Blake keeping an eye out now."

Jen shrugged. "I feel better about standing up to him if that's what you mean. Mr. Blake reminds me of my grandfather with his quiet protectiveness. And the officers really did a great job of keeping the situation under control. They didn't let him near me once he left the motel."

"Tell me about the officer that stuck around. Officer Richards, was it?" Maureen let a small smile creep across her face. She knew Paul from his teen years. He came from a troubled home, but let it push him into a better future.

Jen felt her cheeks flush and hoped it wasn't obvious after her crying spell. "He's nice. Very dedicated to his job." She paused before quietly adding, "And not too bad to look at either."

She shook her head and looked at Maureen, who was making a quick note on the notepad. "He took me to dinner the night Andrew was arrested."

Maureen stopped her pen mid sentence and looked up at Jen. "Like a date?"

Jen laughed, "No, not like a date. More of a *let's get a warm meal* type of thing. He took me to dinner for comfort food and coffee," she sighed and continued, "A true gentleman if I do say so myself." She smiled again at the memory and let her thoughts drift to their conversations during dinner.

Maureen cleared her throat, bringing Jen back to the present. "I'm sure he was. I've never known Paul to be anything else." The confusion on Jen's face was obvious, so she continued, "Paul and I go way back to when he was a teenager. He did yard work for me in exchange for advice. That's about all I can say without breaching confidentiality."

Jen nodded, showing her understanding. "Of course," she mumbled as she sat up a little straighter and snapped her rubberband.

Maureen made another tally for this session. Jen was up to eight so far, and they'd only been sitting for about thirty minutes. "What made you snap your rubberband that time? Was it triggered by talking about Paul or by a thought about the other night with Andrew?" At this point, Jen's wrist was turning red.

Jen slid her finger under the band and pulled it away from her skin. She didn't snap it, though. "I'm not sure, to be honest with you. I think it was me realizing that I'm going to have to talk about Andrew more. I'm clearly not past it all yet."

Maureen pursed her lips and shifted in her seat. "Jen, it will be a long time before you're over it all. Every man will be compared to Andrew. Every touch will make you flinch, at least for a while. It will be so hard for you to have a relationship where trust is easily given. It won't be easy or quick, but it will come if you let it."

She watched as Jen wiped away a single tear. Maureen knew Jen had reached her peak for this session. "We can end for today if you'd like. I want to try something different before our next session if that's okay with you." She waited for Jen to reply. All she got was a small nod. "I'd like for you to write some of these memories down. Here's a notebook for you to use. And a black pen. Only use black." She handed the items to Jen.

"Why black?" Jen asked as she flipped the pen between her fingers like a tiny baton.

"Black is a color that represents anger, aggression, fear, and sadness. But it's also a color used for power, strength, and authority. I'm hoping that you will be able to release some of the negative feelings by writing them. And by seeing them in black, maybe it will hold a sense of finality. Besides, I think it would be easier than talking about everything. Sometimes words come out more easily through a pen than out loud."

Jen smiled and stood. "I think you might be onto something, Maureen. This notebook might be full by next week."

The two women silently made their way to the lobby as they normally did. Only this time, they were met by Mr. Blake.

CHAPTER 8

A Little Low...

Mr. Blake met Jen's confused look with a hard stare.

"Let's get back into the office if that's okay with you ladies. I'm not so sure we are out of harm's way in here." He ushered them back from the lobby and into the security of Maureen's office.

"Mr. Blake, what's going on?" Jen was now starting to panic at the mention of a threat. "Is...is Andrew out? Did he hurt you?" By this point, Jen was starting to get angry. Mr. Blake had become like family to her since she came here. She'd be damned if Andrew would get away with harming him.

Mr. Blake looked over his shoulder one more time before answering, "He hasn't hurt me, but he is out of jail. Paul called earlier and said they couldn't hold him on anything else since his bond had been taken care of. He swears he tried, Miss Jen."

Jen sat on the couch again but felt as if she wasn't really there. All she could think of was the last time Andrew had been released from her pressing charges.

"Do you know what you did to me, Jen?" Andrew looked down his nose at her as she sank back as far as possible into the recliner.

She shook her head vigorously but did not dare to say a word. Andrew was so mad when he found her trying to get into his phone. She knew he had been seeing someone else again, but she didn't have proof. He must've known she was going to look when he went to shower.

"You made me look like a fool. I have done nothing but keep you in the life you want so much. I work my ass off to give you everything that you have. And what's the thanks I get for it? A pair of cheap cuffs and a domestic violence record." He shoved the chair back with such force that Jen thought it would flip right over.

She was tired of him always blaming these things on her. She wasn't the one at fault here for anything other than trying to snoop. Jen felt a surge of bravery burst from her chest. She leapt from her seat and shoved Andrew backward, causing him to tumble onto the couch.

She felt the anger continue to rise as she spat in his face. A decision she immediately regretted.

Andrew grabbed Jen by the shoulders and slung her to the

floor, causing her to hit her head on the hope chest she had been filling with baby things. Her vision grew dark around the edges, making her think she was about to pass out. A wave of nausea washed over her as she was hoisted to her feet and dragged to the bathroom.

She felt herself being dropped into the bathtub and heard the water being turned on. The sound was followed by cold water rushing over her. Andrew had dumped her in the tub and tried to wash away her panic attack.

Fortunately for Jen, the shock of the water brought her back to her senses. She pulled her face from the flow of water and coughed harshly, pushing the water from her lungs. This wasn't as bad as the time he held her head over the toilet and dumped a bucketful over her, but still alarming nonetheless.

Andrew shoved her head back under the falling water and started to ask, "Why are you making this out to be my fault, Jen? I've done nothing but love you and give you everything you need. Say it's not my fault. Take the blame like you should!"

He turned the water off and wrapped a towel around her head, scrubbing it over her face. Jen felt her body start to slide into the darkness that crept over her earlier and gave in to it this time.

Darkness...no more pain...silence... Finally, she was at peace.

Jen felt a gentle shake on her shoulder that brought her back to the present. Maureen and Mr. Blake both stared at her with concern. Although Mr. Blake was in the dark about most of her past, Maureen seemed to know exactly what happened.

"It's okay, Jen. He won't ever hurt you again if I have anything to do with it." Maureen pulled out her cell phone and dialed the local sheriff's office. "Hi, I don't have an emergency...yet, but I need to see if Officer Richards can do a wellness check at my office." She finished the phone call with a quick *thanks* and squeezed Jen's hand. "Paul is coming as quickly as he can. Believe it or not, this type of thing happens sometimes here, and he's my go-to for handling it."

Jen laid her head on Maureen's shoulder and gave a shuddering breath. Mr. Blake looked through the front blinds in time to see Andrew ride by in his truck. Luckily, he hadn't figured out that she was there yet. Not long after, Paul pulled up and knocked on the door with a sort of code.

Tap, Tap, Knock, Tap Knock.

Maureen kept the shades drawn while letting Paul in and quickly shut the door again.

Paul saw Jen and instantly knew the issue he was responding to. "Miss Ashworth, I promise I'm trying to find grounds to get him out of town. He hasn't stopped at the motel or anywhere else for that matter. He's just...riding." He looked distraught that he wasn't able to do much more.

Jen gave a half smile and brushed her fingers over Paul's shoulder. "It's Jen, please." It seemed as if they both felt the jolt of the touch, as small as it was. "I appreciate it all, and I don't expect you to do more than you are legally obligated to do. I just want peace and for him to leave me alone."

Maureen and Mr. Blake looked at one another, noticing the small gesture between the two. Their looks both seemed to say *this could be good*.

Mr. Blake looked over at Paul, seeing the familiar longing in his eyes. "Paul, can I speak to you for a moment?" He held out a hand to lead him from the office area back to the lobby.

"Mr. Blake, I know you're worried about your place and the other patrons. I promise I'm doing all I can to..." Mr. Blake cut Paul off with a hand on his shoulder.

"Paul, I can see just how smitten you are right now with Miss Jen. I can assure you, I will be just fine looking over my place. Keep her safe and get that bastard out of town." Paul started to protest but was cut off again. "She's a great girl. A little battered and broken, but great nonetheless. She needs to know that she's safe here." Mr. Blake patted his shoulder again and turned to walk back to Jen and Maureen.

Paul stood alone for a bit, not sure how Mr. Blake could tell he was taken aback by Jen's presence. Their coffee and dinner the other night was one that he really enjoyed. Her company would be nice to have around. "I'll do my absolute best," Paul whispered to himself as he walked back out the front door.

Mr. Blake made his way over to the women and cleared his throat. With his hands in his pockets and rocking back on his heels, he looked Jen directly into her eyes. (An odd gesture coming from him.) "Miss Jen, I will drive you back to your room and keep a close eye out. You're more than welcome to stay in the office with me until we are all certain what's his name won't be stopping by." He looked down at his shoes and felt his cheeks flush.

Jen hugged him gently and thanked him for the offer. "I promise to be quiet and stay out of your way if you allow me to cook dinner for us. I'll make an old favorite, meatloaf and homemade mashed potatoes." She hooked her arm into his and waved goodbye to Maureen.

They all knew Jen was in good hands with Mr. Blake. He had taken up a grandfatherly role since the day she came into town. No better gentleman had been there to help since she started dating Andrew. It felt nice to have people that actually showed they cared.

They got in the car and made their way back to the motel for a quiet afternoon and hot meal.

CHAPTER 9

Meeting Natalie...

Jen made her way around Mr. Blake's kitchen, looking for the ingredients needed to cook their dinner. It was the least she could do after he had stuck himself out so far for her safety. While the potatoes boiled, she used the Alexa to play some soothing music. It usually helped to calm her nerves after a long day, and this surely qualified as that.

The current song playing was an instrumental cover of "River Flows in You" by Hauser. Jen found herself humming along to the tune, slowly forgetting that she was supposed to be on her toes with Andrew still around.

Mr. Blake rounded the corner from the office, making sure to announce his presence so as not to startle Jen. "Something smells good, Miss Jen. Is there by any chance enough for three?" There he goes, rocking on his heels again and not making eye contact.

Jen smiled with adoration and replied, "There certainly is,

Mr. Blake. Are you expecting company?"

He shook his head and sighed. "I hope you don't mind, but my niece Natalie is in town and wanted to meet for dinner. I told her you had already started cooking and invited her over to enjoy the meal with us. I promise there will be no talk of houses unless you bring it up."

"Meeting her would be nice. Especially since she seems to be so close to you." She stirred the gravy and tapped the side of the pot. "About how far out is she? This should all be ready in about twenty minutes."

"Knock knock! I hope you don't mind my letting myself in. I still have my key." A whirlwind of a young woman tossed her bag and sweater on the couch and wrapped Mr. Blake in a giant hug. "Uncle Owen. It's so good to see you."

Mr. Blake smiled, the biggest Jen had ever seen from him.

"Nattie, my girl. How's life treating you?" He returned the hug and ushered her towards the sofa. As they sat, he motioned for Jen to join them. "This is Jen Ashworth. She's the kind young lady that's been helping out on her days off."

"It's so nice to finally meet you, Natalie. I've heard so much about you." The two shook hands, and Jen joined the duo from the chair in the corner. She didn't want to intrude, but then again, Natalie knew she would be there.

"It's nice to meet you, also, Jen. My uncle here seems to be very happy that you're around these days. I hear you make him mind his manners and keep the cats around." She winked at Jen as Mr. Blake shook his head.

"Enough with formalities. Is it time to eat, Miss Jen? I'd hate to let good food go to waste." He made his way to the kitchen, leaving the women behind.

Natalie squeezed Jen's hand and whispered, "Thank you for taking care of him. He's also really enjoyed your company."

The two joined him in the kitchen and made their plates. The dining table was small but just right to fit the three of them comfortably. The three ate the majority of their dinner in silence, only giving the occasional *mmm* to note their satisfaction.

Once everyone had finished eating, Mr. Blake offered to do the dishes and bring out slices of cake for dessert.

Jen cleared her throat, hoping now was as good a time as any to approach the subject of houses. "Natalie, Mr. Blake says that you have a few houses that would possibly be affordable for someone in my current situation. I haven't had the chance to look over any of them myself, but I'd like to know more about them if you have the time one day soon."

"I have a few in different ranges depending on what you're looking for. If you want a fixer-upper, I can get you a decent price. Something a little more move-in ready would obviously run a bit higher. Do you have a budget in mind of what you'd be able to afford?" Natalie paused, "I don't mean to sound pushy; I'm just trying to get a feel for what you want. Does that make any sense?"

"It definitely does. Budget-wise, I don't have much to offer. I'm on a small income from waiting tables and tips. I don't have many bills other than my phone and a weekly session with a therapist that your uncle put me in touch with. And, of course, the room fee here. But that's not much considering other places." Jen shrugged, not knowing what exactly to say in response to Natalie's questions.

Natalie stood, "I'll be right back. Let me go grab my laptop so I can show you what I have available."

Mr. Blake stepped to the side to let Natalie pass and placed the cake plates on the table. "Is she leaving already?" He sat back in his usual seat.

"No, sir, she's just going to get her laptop. We are looking at houses." Jen grinned and waited for Mr. Blake to register what she'd just said.

"Ah, I knew you'd end up staying around. You will love

it here if you don't already. Besides, I think someone else also wants you to stick around." He smiled down at his plate without continuing the conversation.

Before Jen could pry, Natalie strolled back in, laptop already open to the webpage.

"So here's what I'm thinking. I have two that are fixer-uppers but are set at really good prices. By fixer-upper, I mean it needs some love and a good coat of paint. Do you want to see those? Or would you rather have move-in-ready?"

Natalie sat and pushed the laptop in Jen's direction.

"I'm perfectly fine with a fixer-upper as long as I can stay in it while I work on it. Honestly, I think I would value it more if I were able to put my own little touches here and there. Other than decor, of course." Jen scrolled the properties on the screen in front of her.

Natalie moved her chair over to sit next to Jen and tapped the image of the one Jen liked the most.

The house was definitely older. The description states it was built in 1875. However, previous owners did some remodeling and kept it looking as good as it could for its age. There are two interior chimneys on each side to heat the home. The floor plan showed a traditional Victorian style with two rooms on either side of the central hall. The windows had been replaced but still looked to suit the style and age of the house itself. The porch was simply beautiful with its columns and latticework. And the bay window…it was perfectly situated to catch the evening sun.

There weren't many interior photos, which Jen assumed was because it needed work, but she fell in love with it nonetheless.

"Can we go look at this one? It has that cozy feel just from the pictures." Jen looked at the images longingly without meaning to.

Natalie smiled and patted Jen's hand. "Of course we can. I am able to take you as early as tomorrow if you'd like to go then."

Jen gave a grin. "I'd love to! I'm actually off tomorrow, so when I finish up cleaning for Mr. Blake, I can meet you somewhere. I am usually done by lunchtime on a good day." She impatiently tapped her foot, hoping that Natalie wouldn't notice her sitting on the edge of her seat.

Natalie gave a nod, and before she could answer, Mr. Blake stepped into the conversation.

"Miss Jen, you are not cleaning for me tomorrow. You need to do this for yourself. Don't worry about the rooms. Besides, I think only three will need it after checkout. I can handle that just fine." He turned to walk off again before looking back. "And you can borrow my car to get there. I won't take no for an answer." With that, Mr. Blake returned to the kitchen to begin washing dishes.

"Well, I guess that's that then." Natalie gathered her things back into her bag. "I'll see you around 9:30 in the morning? Here's my card with the address to my office. I just know you're going to love the home." Natalie hugged Jen tightly before leaving.

Jen turned back to Mr. Blake, sighing. "Thank you so much for doing all of this for me. I hope you don't think it's something I expect. I mean, I truly appreciate it. I just hope it all works out, and I can get back on my feet again."

Mr. Blake handed Jen a towel to start drying the dinner dishes. "Give it to God and let it go. If it's His will, it'll be."

The two finished the dishes in silence as Jen let the thoughts of having her own place again settle into her mind. *God, please let this be my big break.*

CHAPTER 10

All a Blur...

The next few months went by so fast that Jen couldn't seem to keep up. Work picked up, and she brought home more income. The house-buying process was seamless, and Mr. Blake helped move her in. Andrew came by the restaurant once while she was on shift just to talk. Jen made sure she was where everyone could see and hear while she took her break to appease him.

Andrew looked down at his intertwined fingers and sighed. "I know you're not coming back, Jen. I just need the closure that this is what you want. I'm heartbroken and can't believe you would just abandon me like you did. What did I do to deserve it?"

He seemed to really not know...

"Andrew, I lost myself for you. I gave up everything I had to please you. You took it all from me and let me drown in my fears of losing you. You ran around with God only knows how many other women while we were living together and had a pregnancy scare with one of them. So, no. I didn't abandon you. You wrecked me until I was no longer recognizable to anyone, not even myself. I deserve to be happy. And for the first time in years, I am. I can go and do whatever I want without having to worry about you beating me. I can have friends that you aren't able to scare off. I have a home where I don't have to sleep with one eye open. People here care about me. People here are helping me. People here have the purest intentions for my well-being. I can't say the same for you. So, yes. This is what I want. I want to be left alone to live my life and build myself back up. I want to *not* have to cover the bruises with makeup. I want to gain all the weight I lost because of you." Jen paused to let herself calm down. People were starting to notice their disgruntled conversation.

Andrew shook his head and whispered an apology. "I'm sorry, Jen. I know you can do anything on your own. You don't need me or that Barney Fife that's been following you around town. I just don't want to lose you. But it seems like it's too late for that."

Jen stood and crossed her arms over her chest. "That Barney Fife is the man that kept you from hurting me again.

He's a good man that I'll never have to worry about hitting me. It's over, Andrew. It's been over for a while now. I just finally got the balls to leave and stay gone this time."

Jen turned and went back to her shift. She didn't have time to deal with this anymore. She now had her own home, her first real job since she'd started seeing Andrew, and she finally felt free.

Part II

"Blackbird singing in the dead of night
Take these broken wings and learn to fly..."

-Blackbird-
by John Lennon and Paul McCartney
recorded by The Beatles

CHAPTER 11

Starting Over...

Jen walked around the house with her head in the clouds. It was hers. Finally, something she didn't have to fight to keep. She circled the couch in the living room with visions of what she could turn it into manifesting in her mind. A playlist from the nineties was on repeat in the background. For some reason, it helped her center herself. Music from her happier days. The olive green loveseat had to have a place in the end result.

She sat in the left corner that was already sinking from someone claiming that place long ago. The comfort it brought her was unmatchable. Someone loved this spot as much as she did. Someone who had a life that didn't revolve around being someone's punching bag. That's what she told herself anyway. She didn't want to think of anyone else living the life she had up to this point. The pain was more than enough for one person, yet she willingly bore it all.

As she sat, she scrolled through her phone. She found herself on a page talking about narcissism. *Narcissist: a person with an exaggerated sense of self-importance.* The definition itself was all she needed to read. Andrew at his finest. Is any more explanation even needed? She swiped out of the app and dropped her phone on the cushion next to her.

She closed her eyes and scrubbed her forehead with the palm of her left hand. This was what she did when she wanted to wipe out all the bad memories. It never worked, though. Andrew always seemed to make a dark appearance in her mind. She hadn't seen or spoken to him in months, yet he still had a massive presence in her life.

Jen decided to stop being so negative and walked to the kitchen for a glass of her favorite red wine. Natalie had gifted it to her after the closing of the house. She was a good woman, Natalie. She really should keep her around and let the friendship blossom. Someone who had been in a similar situation but still didn't know Jen's full truth. What was it Jen called that in the past? Spirit animals. She gave a snort at the thought.

Sadness and anxiety had no place in her life now. She was determined to make her new accomplishment one that was full of joy. "Alexa, play my hype playlist." At that, Flo Rida blared from the speaker.

Jen danced around the kitchen in her new house. *HER house!* This really was a dream come true. She had never acquired anything on her own, but working tirelessly gave her the boost (and tips) she needed to get her feet firmly planted. She had recently secured a remote job working for an attorney, so funds were starting to stack in her tiny account. Her boss helped her get the loan for the home and told her it was in a great little town to settle.

Safety and stability. That was exactly what she needed.

Jen stopped dancing and sat on the cracked countertop. It gave the place charm, she thought. There were a few things that needed to be fixed, but she could handle it all on her own. She closed her eyes again and let the sounds and smells of the new place take her away.

The flowers blooming on the back porch rails were the sweetest-smelling jasmine she could ever imagine. (Deep breath...) The birds chittering back and forth sounded like heaven to her city ears. (Sigh...) The roses she had placed in a vase by the window over the sink drifted their perfume across her nose. (Deep breath...) Smoke.

Cigarette smoke tainted the smell of the roses and jasmine. Jen's heart pounded, but she didn't dare open her eyes. Had Andrew been able to find her again? Did he somehow get her address this quickly? She snapped her eyes open as wide as she could and looked around with her heart pounding into her ears. The sound of the birds disappeared and was replaced by the sound of a lawn mower.

She made her way to the front porch cautiously, tilted her head to the side, and looked at the strange man cutting her grass. Who was he, and who told him to come?

She stepped down to the last of the steps and crossed her arms over her chest, waiting for him to turn back her way. When he saw her standing there, he stopped the mower and stubbed out the cigarette. He tucked it away in his pocket instead of throwing it down.

"Can I help you with something, sir?" Jen didn't flinch. She wanted to show strength in case the man walking towards her meant to do her harm. I mean, don't all serial killers start out by cutting the grass of their next victim?

He stopped a few feet short and wiped his hands on his jeans. He held out his right arm in order to shake Jen's hand but slowly withdrew it when he realized her confusion.

"I'm Trenton Richards. Trent for short. I heard someone bought this place, and I wanted to clean up the yards before they moved in, but I see I'm a bit too late. I didn't see a car, so

I assumed the place was still empty for now." He tucked his hands in his pockets and rocked back on his heels. "I can stop if you'd like. I don't expect anything for cutting it; I just enjoy the work."

Jen softened her face and held her hand out to Trent. "I'm Jen. I just got here a few hours ago. My car is parked around back where I unloaded my things." Borrowing Mr. Blake's car was still coming in handy. She shook Trent's hand and nodded a greeting. "Please, don't let me stop you from your work. I was just confused, that's all. Back in the city, we don't have strangers do nice things like this."

"Nice to meet you, Miss Jen. If you need any help moving things or doing any other work, just let me know. My dad used to be the town's handyman. I'm just trying to keep his legacy rolling." He turned and started back to his mower, lighting another cigarette along the way.

"Wait," Jen said as Trent turned back to her, "You said Richards. Any relation to Paul?"

Trent nodded and smiled. "I was wondering if you'd met my brother already. He's a good guy. Leads a much straighter life than I ever have, up until recently."

Jen smiled and didn't bother to question. If things continued to go well with Paul, she might get Trent's story at another time. For now, it was time to keep moving forward. Let the demons of the past stay there.

Jen shook her head at her anxiety and was thankful that her heartbeat had finally slowed. She turned and went back in to start putting things away. She didn't have much, but it was just enough for now. Maybe she'd call Natalie to see if she'd like to get lunch one day as a thank-you for making this purchase so quick and painless.

CHAPTER 12

Just a Dream

Jen found herself staring out the window of her new home. How could Adrew have found her again? He swore he would leave her alone, and months later, he's at her driveway waving. What on Earth could he want??

"I think you should leave," Jen whispered, knowing he couldn't hear her.

Andrew smiled, the one grin that made her melt that first time. "I can't do that just yet. You see, I have some unfinished business I need to take up with you." He stepped forward but still didn't move any closer.

Jen tried to step back and shut the door, but some invisible force held her in place. She tried to turn around but couldn't move that way either.

Andrew stepped forward again, this time ending up on her steps and just a few feet away from her. "I need to tell you something that I'm sure you'll want to hear. Just last week, I got hurt at work and had no one to call. Your number is different now, and my family still thinks I'm pulling their legs when I call with a problem." He stepped forward again, this time appearing in the house behind her.

Jen spun around with the force to knock down a wall but couldn't lay a hand on him. Why was this happening to her? How did he have that power over her even now? Tears stung the back of her eyes.

"I just want to tell you something, Jen. I'm not going to hurt you...anymore. I realize all the things I've done wrong and all the ways I've hurt you. You didn't deserve any of it." Andrew looked down at his feet before continuing. "I won't admit this to anyone, so don't try to say this happened. You know I'll deny it with my life. You were the problem for me. You let me get away with everything for far too long, and I buried you with guilt."

Jen couldn't hold back the tears now. They were flowing freely with every shudder of a breath she took. "You took so much from me. I lost who I was, all my friends, my family... I had nothing when I was with you, and I have nothing left with you now. I am building myself back up and making myself better for my future. Nothing you say can make me forget the things that happened. I will forgive your actions because that's what I'm supposed to do. It won't happen anytime soon, but I'll get there one day." Jen raised her shoulders and swiped the tears from her face. "Now, like I said earlier, you need to leave."

Andrew cocked his head to the side and sighed. He held his arms out to his sides and asked, "Can I at least have one last hug?"

Before Jen could respond, Paul stepped out of the kitchen into the room with them. "She asked you nicely to leave. Is there another way of asking that you respond to? Because, as far as I'm concerned, that firmly means get out and don't come back." He crossed his arms over his chest and stood by Jen.

Andrew put his arms down and stepped out onto the porch. "I guess that's my cue. Have a nice life, Jen. You have nothing without me, and you never will." With that, Andrew disappeared.

Jen turned to Paul, noticing that he was fading from existence. "Paul, don't leave me. I need the safety you make me feel. I need the stability you offer just by being in my life. You make me feel whole again." The tears returned.

Paul gave a half-smile and turned back towards the kitchen. "Jen, your strength is inside of YOU. I don't have that stability you crave; you found it when you left Andrew. He doesn't have any power over you anymore. Don't let him hold you back from believing in yourself."

Before Jen could respond, Paul disappeared also.

Jen woke with a yelp and shook her head to clear the images still playing in her mind. Why would she dream that? None of those things had happened, so it's not like it was a memory. Andrew would never apologize and walk away.

And Paul...what was that all about? She slid out of bed and made her way to the bathroom. A good, hot shower would wash away this feeling. Only, she didn't want it to wash away the one seeing Paul made her feel. That one could stay.

CHAPTER 13

When Life Gives You Lemons...

Jen shook the dream from her mind while she continued to clean her new home. Well, it was not so new, being built so long ago, but new to her nonetheless. She had to get things in order with her lender coming by to see the progress. She didn't know who the miracle person was, but someone accepted her request and gave her a chance. She would do everything in her power to show them she was true to her word.

She had just finished sweeping the last bit of the living room when she heard voices outside. She could only see the car from the window, which she recognized as Natalie's. She hid the broom in the closet and dusted off her shirt. It was a bit wrinkled from working, but it wouldn't matter. Maybe it would solidify that she had been the one to put in all the effort to make this house her home.

Jen opened the door to welcome Natalie and her lender, but she only had Mr. Blake with her.

"Oh," Jen hesitated, "I wasn't expecting company, Mr. Blake. I'm a mess, but the house is tidy." She dusted off her shirt again. "Natalie, I thought the lender would be with you today. Did something come up?"

Mr. Blake stepped forward with an outstretched hand. "Miss Jen, I'm your lender." He let his smile crinkle his eyes as he held back what looked to be tears. "You see, I was the seller of this property. It has been in my wife's family for ages. When she passed away, it was left up to me what to do with it. I knew I couldn't fix it up, so my only option was to sell this place. It just so happened to be around the same time you came into my motel like a whirlwind."

Jen grabbed his hand and held it clasped in both of hers. "Mr. Blake, why didn't you say something?"

"Well, from the very beginning, I could tell you weren't one to accept help without expecting a hefty price tag attached to it. I knew if I told you the house was mine, you'd back out of my offer to finance it for you. Think of it as a rent-to-own. No strings attached; I just need to see it taken care of. That way, I can uphold my promise to my wife." With that, Mr. Blake let a single tear slide down his cheek.

"Mr. Blake, I owe you so much more than I can ever repay. Not only did you take me in and let me stay at your motel for way too long, you gave me the opportunity to work for my stay. That, in turn, led me to find myself again and turn everything back around. This arrangement couldn't be any better now that I know it's yours. Even more of my love and devotion will go into bringing it back to life." Jen also let a lonely tear fall from her eye as she hugged Mr. Blake.

She was more than shocked when he returned that hug instead of shifting on his heels at the slightest touch.

Mr. Blake sighed and pulled back, "Now, do you mind if I look around?"

"Not at all! Please, take your time and feel free to give me some ideas of what it used to look like way back when." Jen stepped back and motioned for them to come inside. "Some of the furniture that was left is still here. Especially the couch."

She followed them inside and watched as Mr. Blake seemed to reminisce. He went through all the rooms, touching the curtains and some old artwork. He stopped at the living room doorway and covered his mouth with his hand.

"It's still here. This couch... You kept it in here." He turned towards Jen and Natalie with wide eyes.

The two women exchanged a questioning glance as Natalie shrugged.

"Mr. Blake, what's the deal with the couch? I kept it because I loved the color and cozy feel of it," she paused before sitting and patting the cushion next to her. "And it's already broken in." She let a giggle slip as Mr. Blake sat beside her.

He took a deep breath and sank deep into the olive green cushions. "This is the very place I sat when I asked her father for her hand in marriage. It's also the very place where I waited for her to come home from work that day. And when she saw me, she knew. I didn't even have to ask. We'd talked about it for months about how we wanted it to be. She just didn't think it would be so soon. I told her the Summer Solstice was the perfect time for our new beginning. *Our* beginning...and that's just what it was. We went to the festival and danced the night away." Tears fell freely as he told the story.

Natalie stepped forward and perched on the arm of the couch. "Uncle Owen, I had no idea this home held so many memories for you. You rarely talk about Aunt Janice anymore. I'm glad you were able to reach this conclusion and keep that promise to her."

Jen swiped at her eyes with the back of her hand. "That's the most beautiful story I've heard in a long time. If you want the couch, Mr. Blake, you are more than welcome to take it. I'll get Paul to help me deliver it for you."

"No, no...you keep it here. This is where it belongs. And who knows, maybe you will have the same memories in this very spot one day." Mr. Blake stood, "Now, if I'm not mistaken, isn't tonight the Summer Solstice Festival?"

The women exchanged glances again and nodded their heads yes.

"Then I guess you both better get ready. Maybe Natalie's new beginning will finally be a baby for me to spoil." he nudged her on the shoulder and grinned from ear to ear.

"Now, Uncle Owen, you know Lucas and I are waiting for the right time," she winked, "but you may be on the right track."

Jen watched the exchange with a sense of longing. "Who knows, maybe this season of lemons will soon be turning to lemonade for me also. It's already a good bit sweeter."

The group made their way out onto the porch again and parted ways. Jen looked down at her phone to check the time and saw a text from Paul.

Paul: *I was wondering if you would be at Solstice tonight. There's something I want to show you.*

Jen: *I was actually just about to ask if you were going. I will meet you there if that's okay. I don't want to impose.*

Paul: *Totally fine! I'll meet you at the town center at 7:00.*

Jen: *See you soon!*

Oh, what to wear! Jen thought to herself as she rushed to get ready for her...date?

CHAPTER 14

Summer Solstice Is Upon Us...

Jen walked to the center of the town, keeping an eye out for Paul. There were so many people out and about. She didn't know so many people could fit in one tiny town square. She stood in place and spun in a slow circle, taking it all in. The sights, the smells, Paul...there he was. A wide smile stretched across her face as he made his way towards her.

"There you are. You look beautiful, by the way. Blue is definitely your color." He watched with close examination as Jen's cheeks turned a deeper shade of pink. "Do you mind taking a walk with me before we visit the vendors?"

"I don't mind at all. I'm a little curious as to what you want to show me when this is all around us." They easily fell into step beside each other.

Paul took Jen to the dock that reached out over the lake. It was probably the most secluded place he could get her to during the festival. She seemed to have a lot on her mind, and he wanted to question her, but he chose silence instead. He reached for her hand, but she only allowed a brush of their fingers before crossing her arms.

"Would it be okay if I fessed up to only wanting to get you alone so we could talk for a bit?" Paul shyly asked.

Jen laughed but nodded her agreement. "I had no idea this was such a big deal. Some time alone is fine with me." Jen turned her back towards the water and leaned into the corner of the dock railing. "So, Paul, tell me why this Summer Solstice festival is so important to the town. I thought it was some kind of pagan ritual or something." She let the look of curiosity flash in her eyes. Not to put a damper on the evening, but she didn't want to participate in a ritual.

Paul smirked and leaned himself into the opposite corner of the dock. "Well, it *is* a pagan ritual, but it means something different here. Our town was founded by immigrants from Ireland. They brought the festival over when they settled. Over the years, we've continued the festival without the pagan rituals." He reached into his back pocket and pulled out a flyer, knowing Jen would ask something along these lines. "This will probably explain it a little more clearly than I can." He held the paper out to Jen and waited for her to take it.

Jen folded the flier and passed it back to Paul. "I like the idea of rebirth. Sometimes your soul needs it in order to move on from past hurt and trauma." She hesitated before lifting herself from the safety of her corner of the dock. "I know I haven't been very forthcoming with my past, but I do want you to know that I'm working on it. I'm working on me." She stood directly in front of Paul, looking into his eyes without wavering. "You don't have to stick around for it, but I'd like for you to. You give me the peace I crave and help me center myself when the world is working against me. I know we haven't known each other that long, and it scares the shit out of me, but it just feels like everything is going to be okay when I'm with you."

Before Jen could continue, Paul took a step towards her and cupped her face in his warm, calloused hands. "Miss Ashworth, it can be days, weeks, or months, and I'd still feel the same way about you. You don't have to tell me anything about your past. Even if you did, it wouldn't change anything. You're amazing, and I want to spend all the time I can with you." Paul paused and let his eyes rest on her mouth. He didn't move in for a kiss but continued to speak instead. "I don't want to scare you away by things moving too fast. I want us to take our time and learn to love again at our own pace. We both have our demons to fight with. I'm just glad I get to fight alongside you." At this, he leaned in for that kiss he so desperately craved.

When the two broke apart, their quick breathing was the only sound they could hear. The sky started to sparkle with the promise of bonfires and festivities. Jen rested her head on Paul's shoulder and sighed, "Let's go join the rest of the town so I can get the full experience of this Summer Solstice." She held tight to his hand as they made their way to the town square.

The bonfire was already blazing when they rounded the

corner. People were all over the place dancing, singing, and just being happy together. Signs were pointing to the different parts of the festival. The Celtic dancing was to the left of the square, next to the pub. The pagan aspect of it was to the right of the square for those who wanted to have a more specific celebration for the festival they knew as *Lithia*. Food trucks and tents were at another corner, as well as crafts, arts, and jewelry focused on the Irish culture.

It took Jen a moment to take it all in. Her wide eyes glittered with the flames of the fire in front of her. It was as if the four corners of the square represented a different element of life in this little town, and the center of it held the sun. "This is what it's all about. Happiness, laughter, the feeling of being carefree...this is it. I've found where I need to be in order to find myself again." She turned to look at Paul with a newfound confidence. "I found my rebirth. And it's all because of the people here. Thank you, Paul. Thank you for understanding my silence and my personal walls. Thank you for just being there when I needed another warm body in the room. Thank you for...this."

Paul wrapped Jen in a tight hug and just held her. He had no idea what battle she was fighting in her heart, but he was glad to be a stepping stone in getting her away from it.

No other words needed to be spoken by the two. They smiled and held on to each other like it was their last night together. The people around them disappeared as the warmth of the fire surrounded them. The only thing they could see was each other. The only thing they could feel was their arms wrapped ever so tightly around each other. The magic of the solstice was floating through the air.

Dear Jen

Dear Jen,

I'm writing this letter to you because Maureen says I need to. She says it's the final step in healing. But what does she know, right? I mean, she only has a doctorate to help people with their hellish lives.

Anyway, you made it. You have made your way out of the darkest days of your life. You dealt with the devil himself and still stood. Look at you!

Enough of me being snarky…

I'm proud of you. You had one of the worst seasons of your life. You put up with a hell of a lot from someone who didn't deserve you. You let him belittle you to no end. He broke you until you didn't recognize yourself, and you made it out alive. There were times when I thought you wouldn't. Times that I thought you'd give up altogether. Those days were the darkest. Hospital visits for erratic heart rates, chest pains, unexplained gashes, and bruises…and you lost *so much weight*.

The best thing you ever did was leave. It may have also been the hardest, but it saved your life, and you know it. You hid the cuts and scratches really well. Your sleeves were always just long enough, and the cardigan you wore all summer because you were cold was easily explained. Yet no one questioned it. The bruises were strategically placed by the one who broke you so others wouldn't suspect anything. Everyone watched you die inside. Some encouraged you to stay and "wait it out."

You tried.

God knows you tried.

You still snap the rubberband, but it's become more of a habit now than a coping mechanism. You don't know you're doing it until it pops and needs replacing. Paul tried to hide them all from you, but he didn't win that one. ☺ He understands, though. He is your angel in disguise. No one else would even try to comprehend all that you've been through.

There are two sides to every story, but people always believe the one they want. It doesn't make it the truth or even remotely honest. They just go with the one they want to believe and make the other party the one in the wrong. There were so many people that were against you because of Andrew.

I feel silly writing this letter to myself. Tell me why we pay Maureen so much money for this shit again?

I kid... She's amazing. She figured out all of your quirks

without you even knowing.

437 times. That's how many tallies she made in the past few months of sessions. The good part is that they are not as frequent now. Who knows, maybe you'll be able to give up the rubberbands altogether soon.

(Yeah, right...)

Time to finish this up. I feel silly... Like I said, I'm proud of you. You left a toxic relationship with nothing to your name and made it! YOU have your own home now. YOU have a car to drive. YOU are working your dream job. YOU have a fantastic support system that YOU created all on your own. YOU DID IT! And you are amazing.

I love you,

Jen Ashworth ♥

Nicole W. Barnes is the talented author behind two beloved romance titles, and "Summer Solstice" marks her eagerly anticipated third novel. When she's not crafting captivating love stories, Nicole leads a fulfilling life as a devoted wife and mother of three. Drawing from her own experiences and boundless imagination, Nicole weaves tales of love, resilience, and hope that resonate with readers worldwide. "Summer Solstice" is sure to enchant romance enthusiasts and newcomers alike, showcasing Nicole's signature blend of heartwarming storytelling and irresistible charm.

Facebook:

https://www.facebook.com/people/Nicole-W-Barnes-Author/100063543035243/

Instagram:

https://www.instagram.com/nicole_barnes6819/

Website:

https://nicolewbarnes.com/